Who's making that smell?

Philip Hawthorn and Jenny Tyler
Illustrated by Stephen Cartwright

 There is a little yellow duck and a white mouse
on every double page. Can you find them?

Who's making that smell?
Pheeeww!!

Behind that screen as well.

It can't be Ben or Annabel.

babbi bubi

It's not me.

Who's making that smell?

POooHH!!

Hey Ben, where's Annabel?

Oh, I can hear her yell.

This edition first published in 2007 by Usborne Publishing Ltd., 83–85 Saffron Hill, London EC1N 8RT, England. www.usborne.com

Copyright © 2007, 2003, 1994 Usborne Publishing Ltd.

The name Usborne and the devices ♨ ⊕ are Trade Marks of Usborne Publishing Ltd. All rights reserved.

No part of this publication may be reproduced, stored in a retrieval system, or transmitted in any form or by any means, electronic, mechanical, photocopying, recording or otherwise, without the prior permission of the publisher.

Printed in China

UE. This edition first published in America 2007